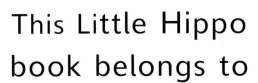

This Little Hippo
book belongs to

_____

_____

For Chris and Nicky
K. L.

Scholastic Children's Books,
Commonwealth House, 1-19 New Oxford Street,
London WC1A 1NU, UK
a division of Scholastic Ltd

London • New York • Toronto • Sydney • Auckland

First published in the UK in 1998 by Little Hippo,
an imprint of Scholastic Ltd

Text copyright © Adèle Geras, 1998
Illustrations copyright © Karin Littlewood, 1998

ISBN 0 590 19577 8

Printed in Italy by Amadeus S.p.A. - Rome

2 4 6 8 10 9 7 5 3 1

The right of Adèle Geras and Karin Littlewood to be identified as
the author and illustrator of this work has been asserted by them in
accordance with the Copyright, Designs and Patents Act, 1988.

ADÈLE GERAS

SUN SLICES, MOON SLICES

Illustrated by
KARIN LITTLEWOOD

Little
Hippo

Every day, Lewis and his mother went to Maria's
house on the bus. Maria looked after Lewis while his
Mum was at work. Every day, Lewis asked his Mum,
"When will you come and take me home?"
Every day his Mum said, "At four o'clock. Give me
a hug and be a good boy till I come and fetch you."

After his Mum had gone, Lewis said to Maria, "When will it be four o'clock?"

"Soon," said Maria, "and even sooner if you play. The time flies when you're happy."

Lewis didn't know if he felt like playing. Daisy and Shena were climbing on the climbing frame. Frankie the cat was watching them.

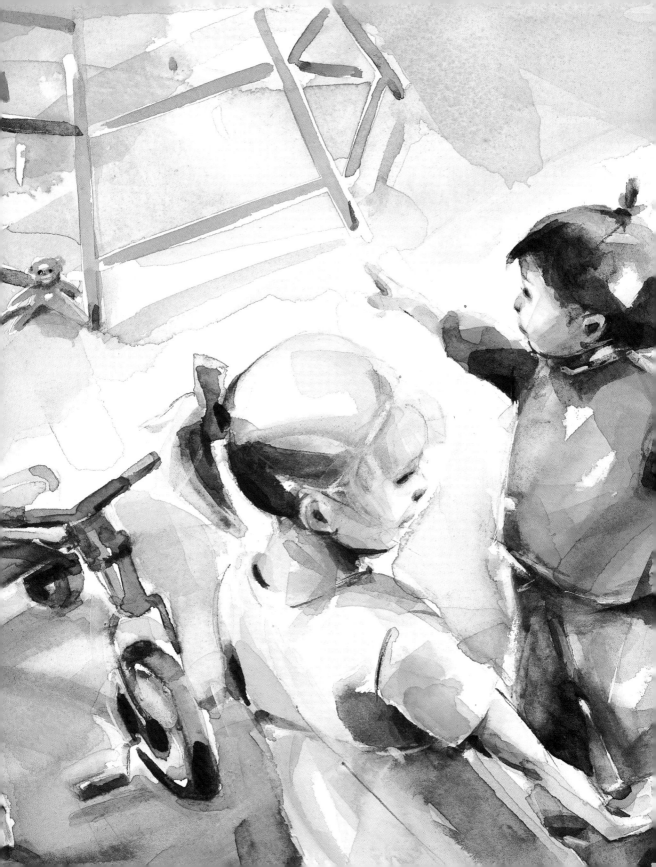

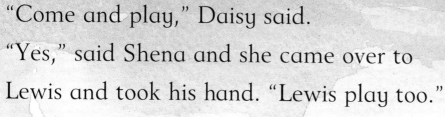

"Come and play," Daisy said.
"Yes," said Shena and she came over to
Lewis and took his hand. "Lewis play too."
Lewis forgot about not wanting to join in.
"This game," Daisy told him, "is called Zoos,
and you can be the zoo-keeper."

Daisy and Lewis wanted Frankie to be the tiger.
They pretended the climbing frame was the tiger's
cage, but Frankie didn't like the game. Lewis put
him in his cage, but he ran straight out of it.

In the kitchen, Maria set the table, ready for lunch. Lewis arranged the forks and spoons and Daisy put out the plates. Frankie sat under the table waiting for tasty bits of food to fall on the floor.

"I wonder," said Maria, "what shall
we have for pudding?"
"Moon slices please," said Lewis.
He always asked for moon slices.
"Sun slices please," said Daisy.
She always asked for sun slices.
"Ice-cream," said Shena and banged
her spoon happily on the table.

Maria cut up an apple. "Here are some pale
green moon slices for Lewis," she said.
Then she cut up an orange. "And here are
some golden sun slices for you, Daisy."
"Eat them slowly and share some with Shena."

Shena poked at the moon slice and sucked at the sun slice, but she liked her ice-cream best.

A large drop of ice-cream fell from Shena's spoon
and landed on the floor next to Frankie.

"Look," said Daisy, "Frankie is licking it up. Frankie loves ice-cream, just like us." Shena laughed.

"You children," said Maria, "have eaten the last apple and the last orange in the fruit bowl so after lunch we'll go for a walk and buy some more." Frankie the cat settled down for a nap under the table.

All the way down the street, Lewis and Daisy took it in turns to push Shena along in her pushchair.

"Is it nearly four o'clock?" asked Lewis.
"My Mum is coming for me at four o'clock."
"Nearly," said Maria, "but now I need you and
Daisy to help me choose some apples and oranges."

Lewis looked at all the apples until he saw some that were as pale green and round as the moon. He put them in Maria's shopping basket. Daisy found four golden oranges. She picked them up and put them in the basket next to the apples. Shena chose a banana.

Maria paid for the fruit and Lewis took one of the bananas. He pretended it was a rocket ship flying through space, right into Shena's hand.

At four o'clock, just as she had promised,
Lewis's Mum came to fetch him. They left
Maria's house together.
"Bye Lewis," said Maria. "See you tomorrow."
"Bye, Lewis," called Daisy. Shena waved.

Lewis and his Mum arrived home. Lewis ran up the stairs to his bedroom and said hello to all his toys.

"I wish Daisy and Shena were here to play with you," Lewis said to them.

Lewis went to find his Mum.
She was in the kitchen,
peeling apples for a pie.
"We always have pie,"
Lewis said. "Why can't
we have moon slices
instead of pie?"

"We will if you tell me what a moon slice is," said
Lewis's Mum.

"Why, don't you know?" asked Lewis. "It's a piece
of apple. Maria calls pieces of apple, moon slices.
Pieces of orange are called sun slices."

Lewis's Mum smiled. "I like those names," she said.

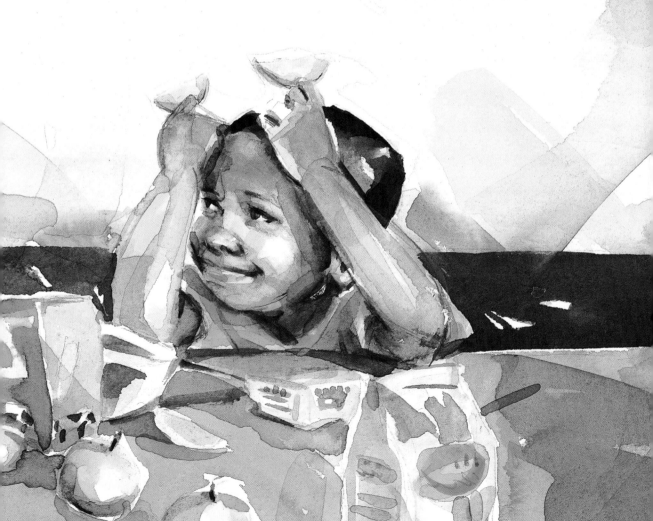

In bed after his story, Lewis said sleepily,
"In the morning, I want to stay with you."
"And I'd like to stay with you," his Mum said,
"but I have to go to work."
"I like playing with Daisy and Shena," said
Lewis, "but I wish they could come to my house.
And I wish Frankie could sleep on my bed."

"Frankie likes his own house," said Lewis's Mum, "and Panda is your night-time friend. He's been waiting all day for his goodnight hug from you, and so have I! Sleep tight, Lewis. Happy dreams."